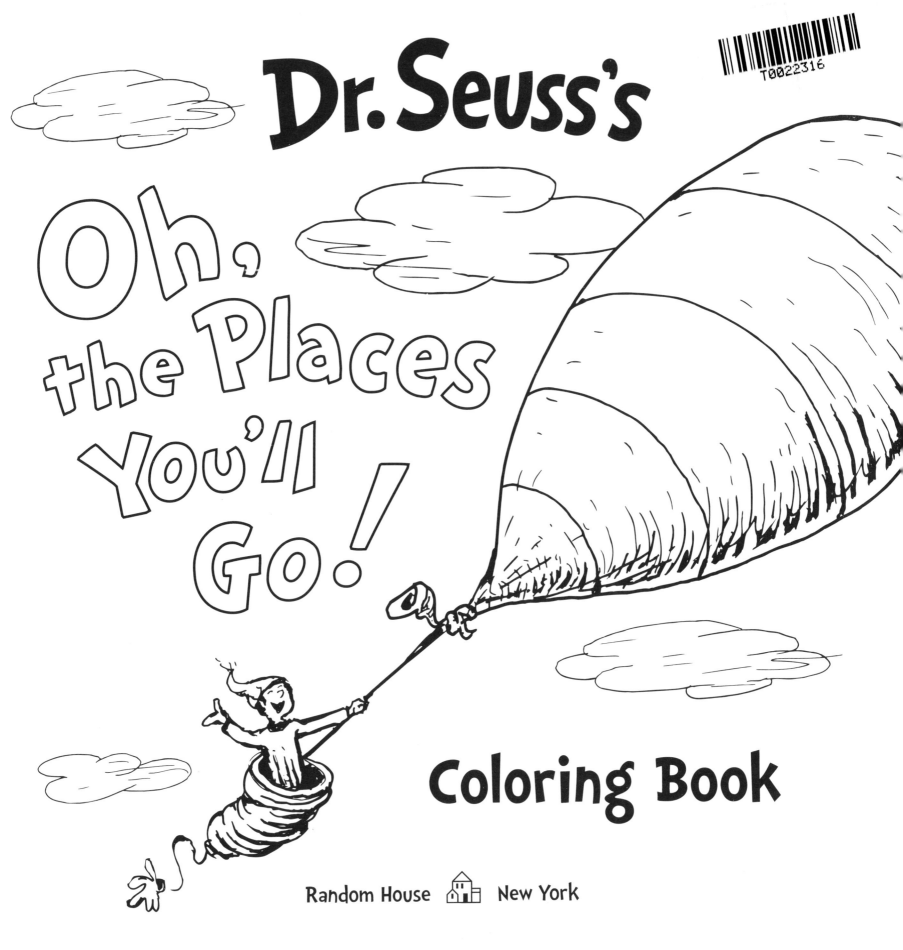

Dr. Seuss's

Oh, the Places You'll Go!

Coloring Book

Random House New York

TM & copyright © by Dr. Seuss Enterprises, L.P. 2020

All rights reserved. Published in the United States by Random House Children's Books, a division
of Penguin Random House LLC, New York. The artwork that appears herein was originally published
in *Oh, the Places You'll Go!,* TM & copyright © 1990 by Dr. Seuss Enterprises, L.P.

Random House and the colophon are registered trademarks of Penguin Random House LLC.

Visit us on the Web!
Seussville.com
rhcbooks.com

Educators and librarians, for a variety of teaching tools, visit us at RHTeachersLibrarians.com

ISBN 978-0-593-37240-1 (trade pbk.)

Printed in the United States of America
10 9 8 7 6 5 4 3 2 1
First Edition

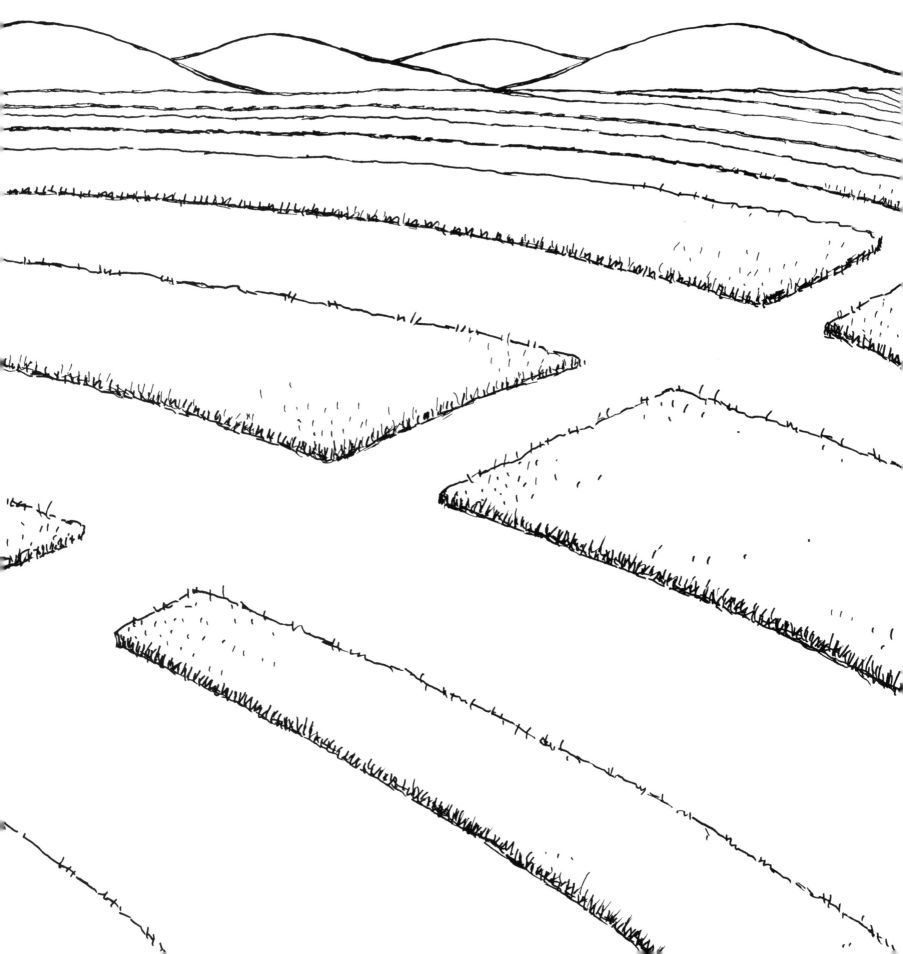

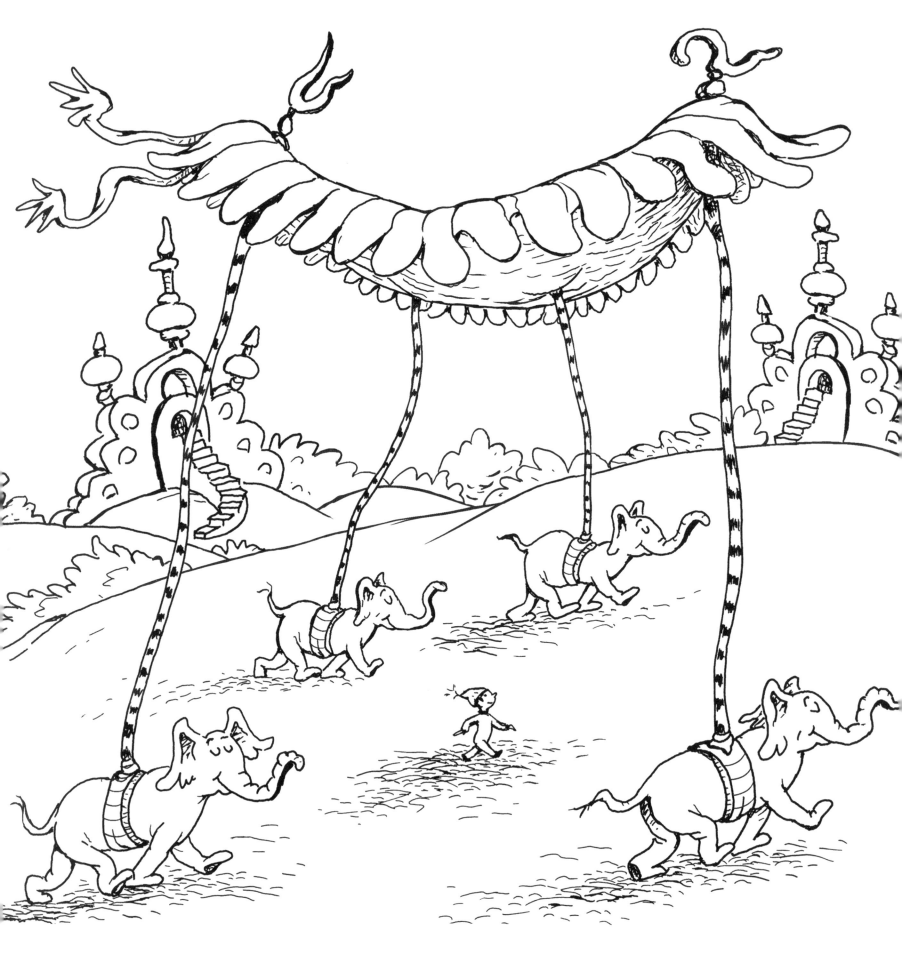

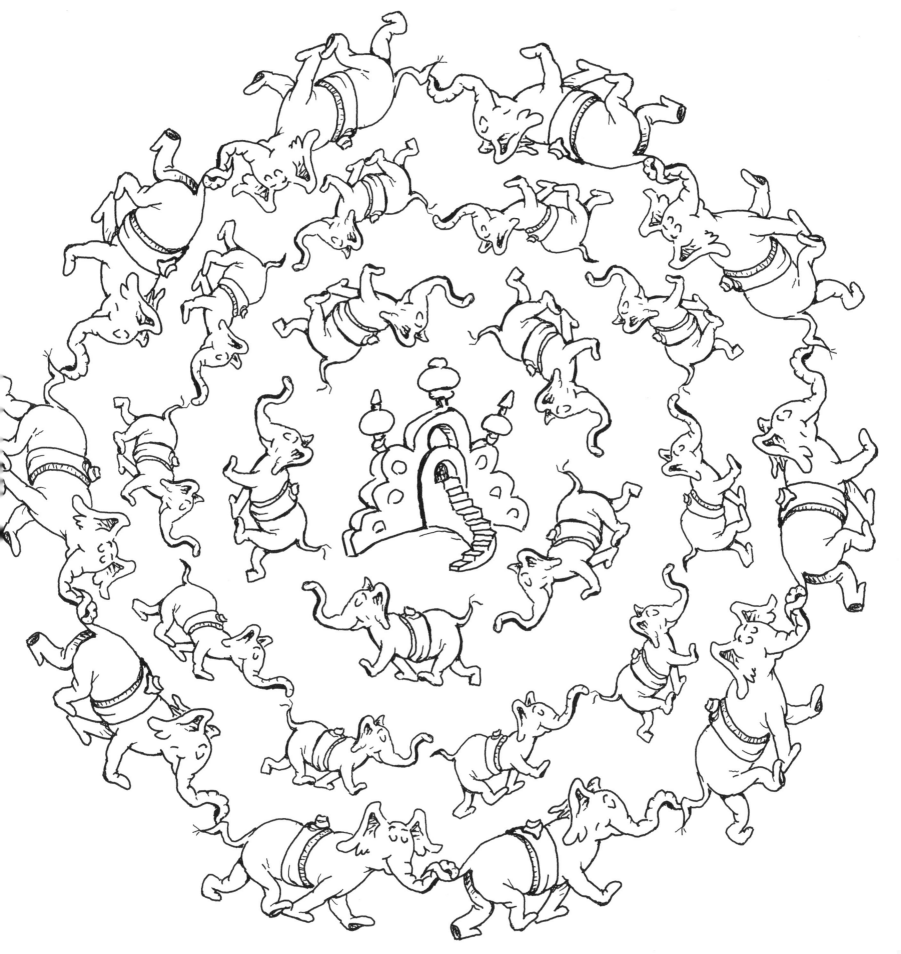

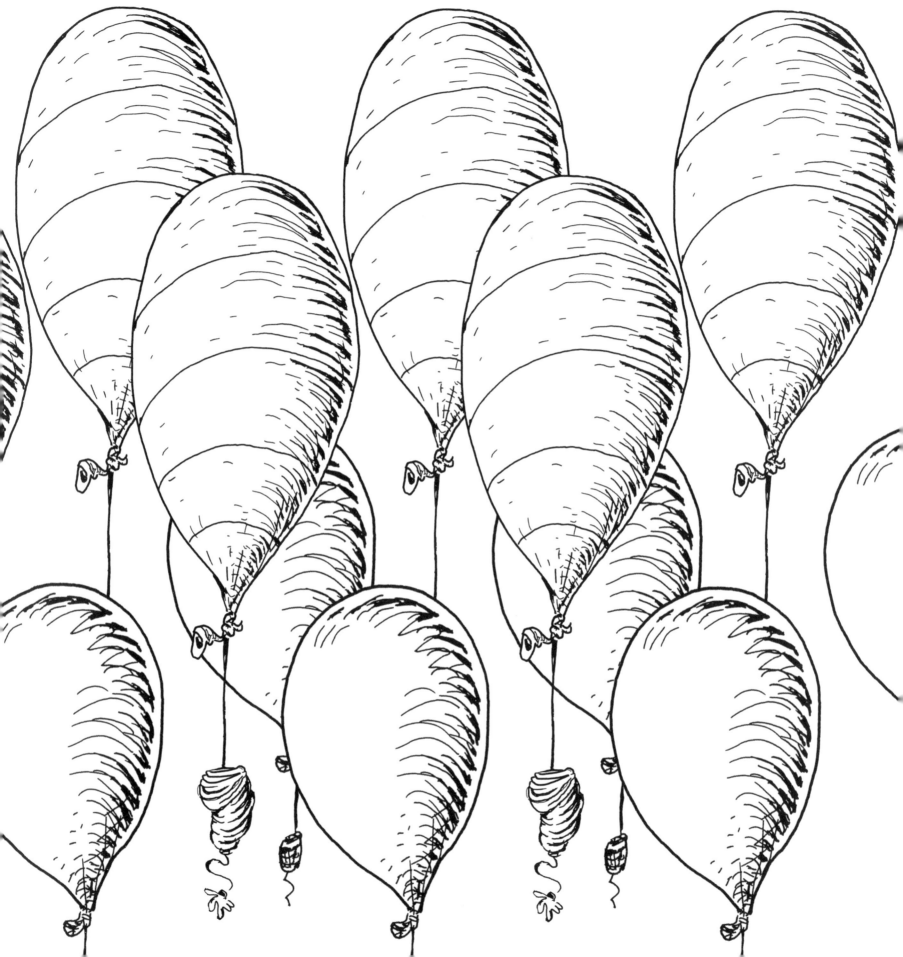

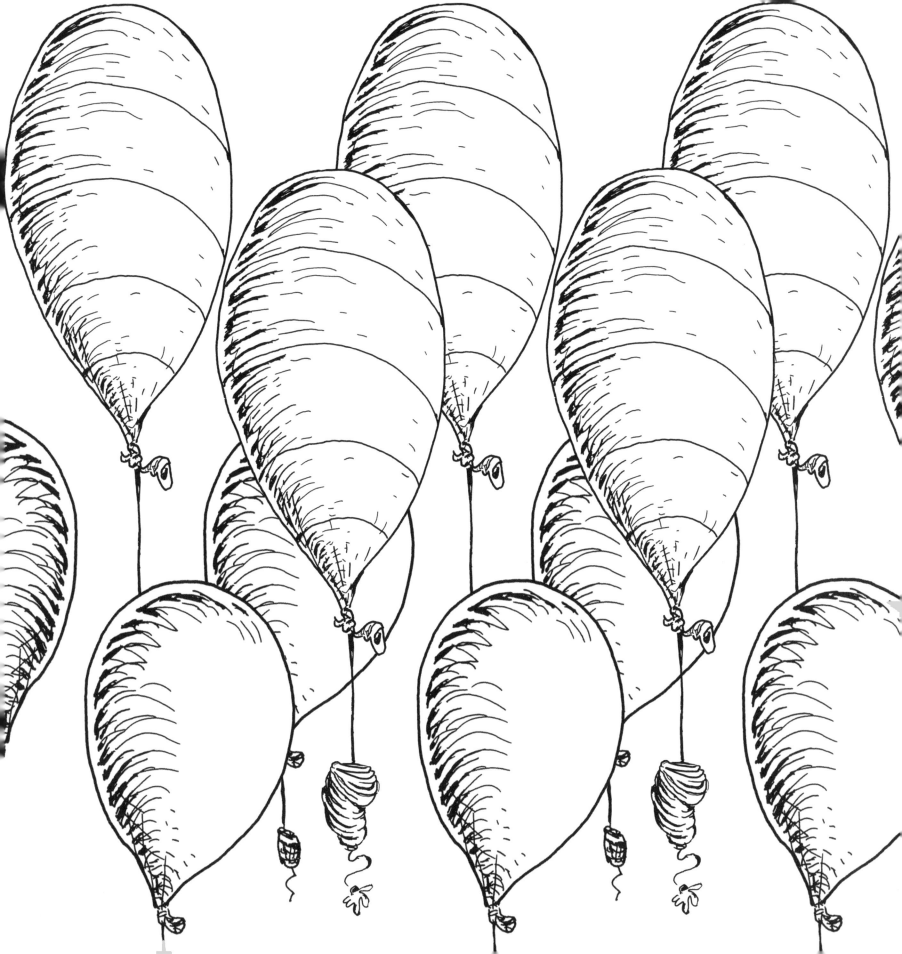

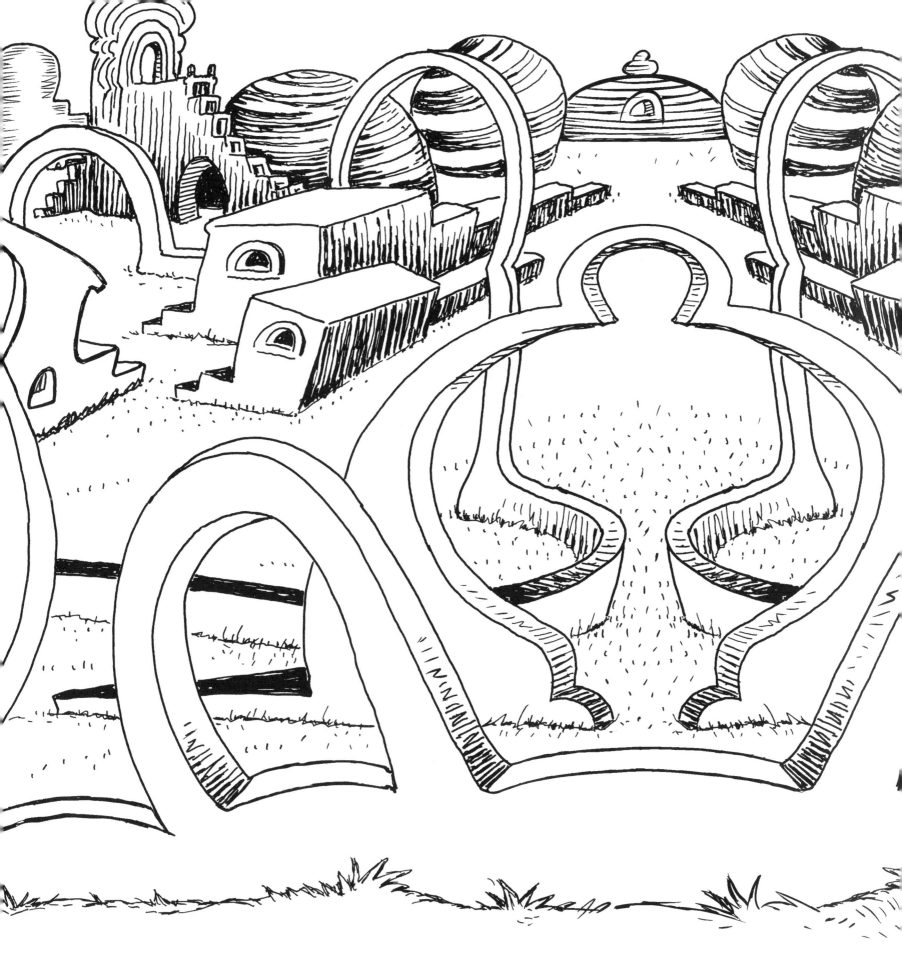

You'll find the bright places where Boom Bands are playing.

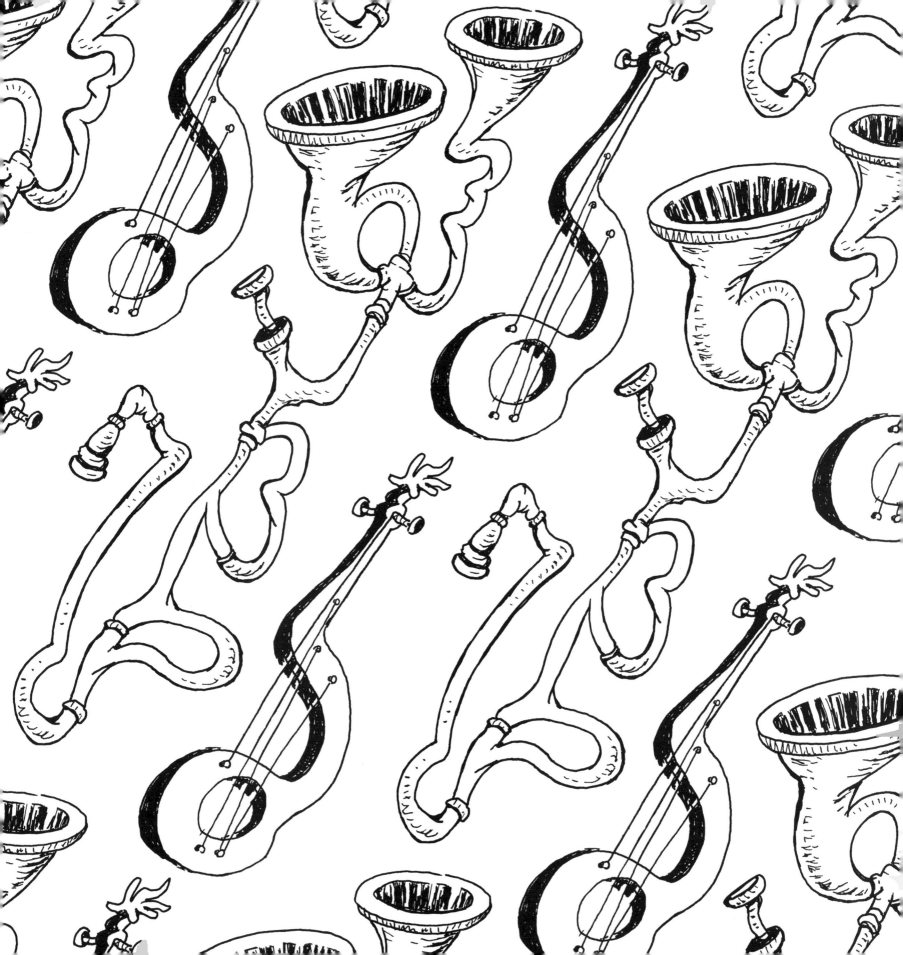

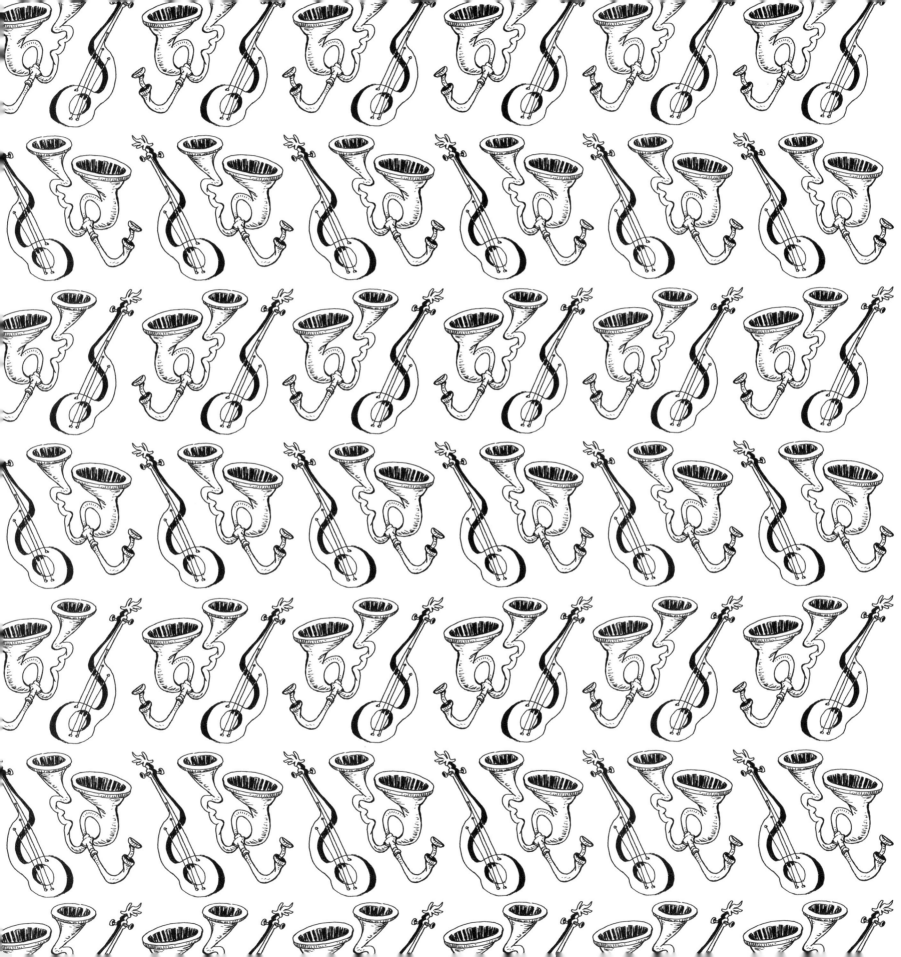

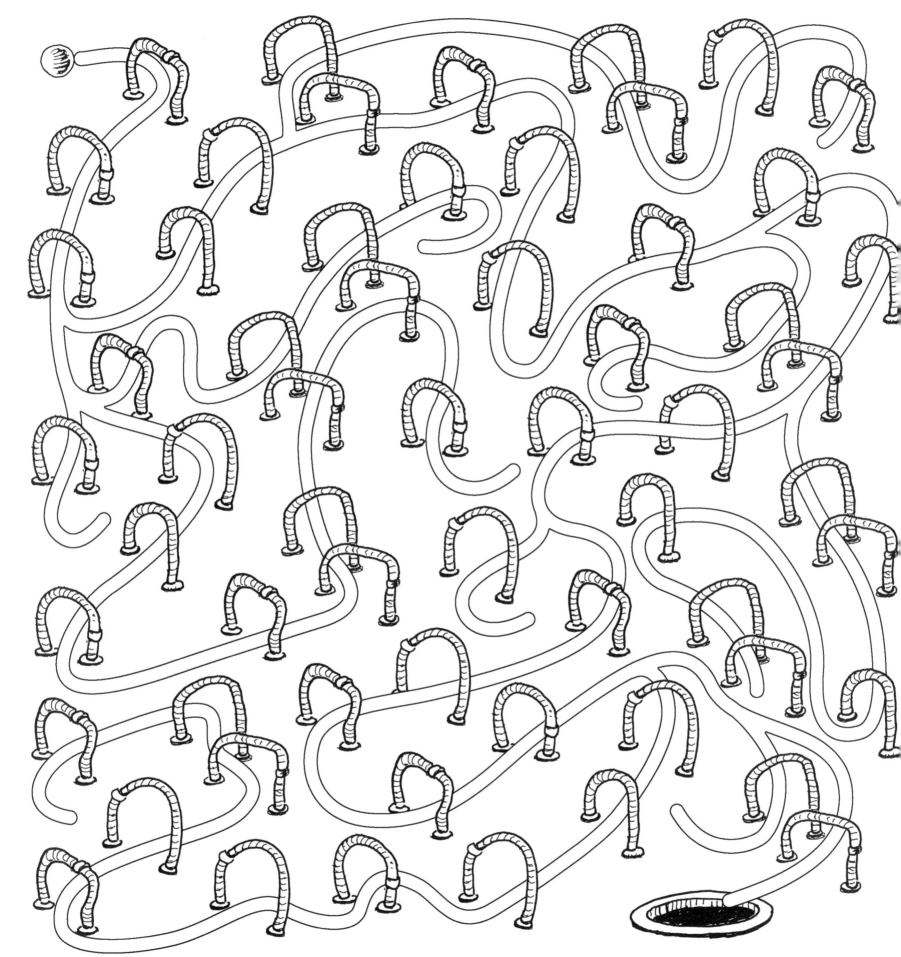

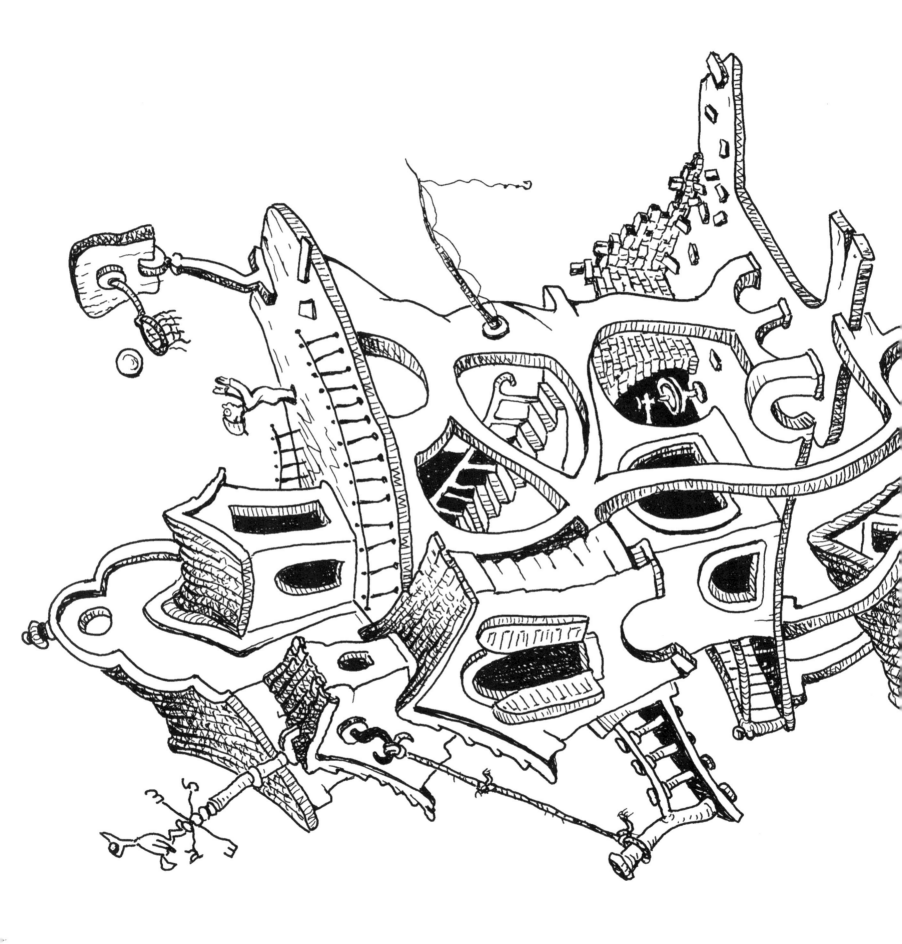

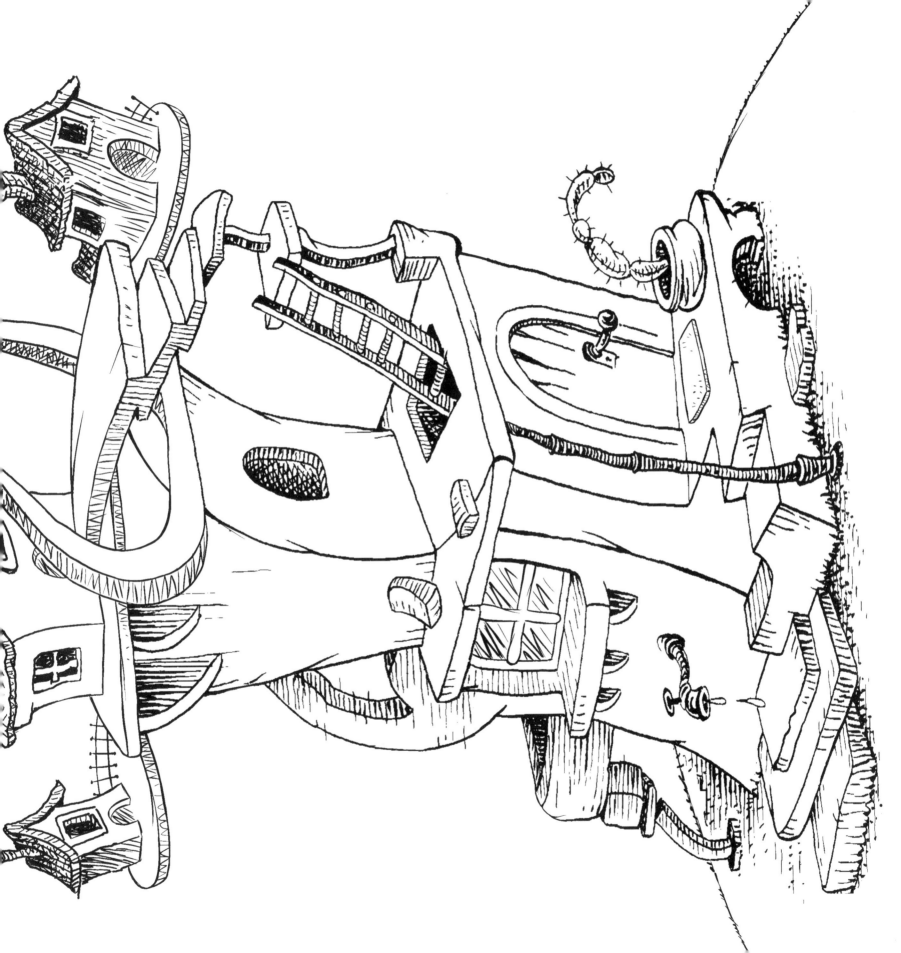

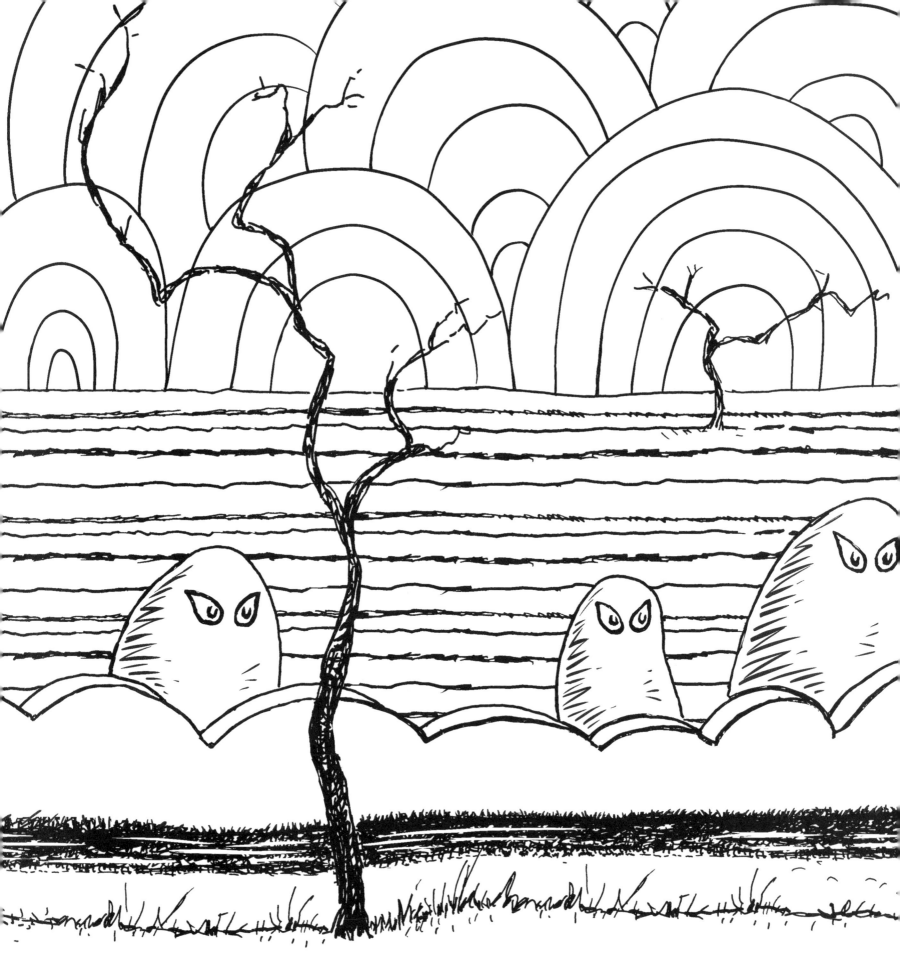

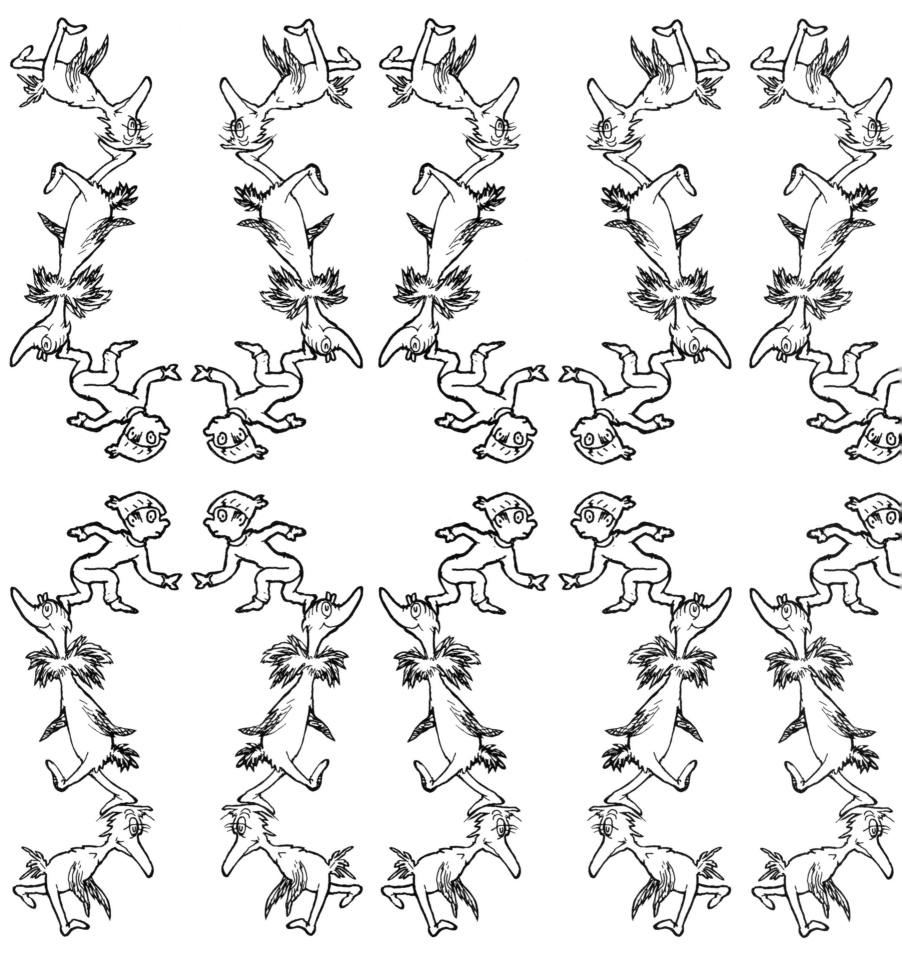

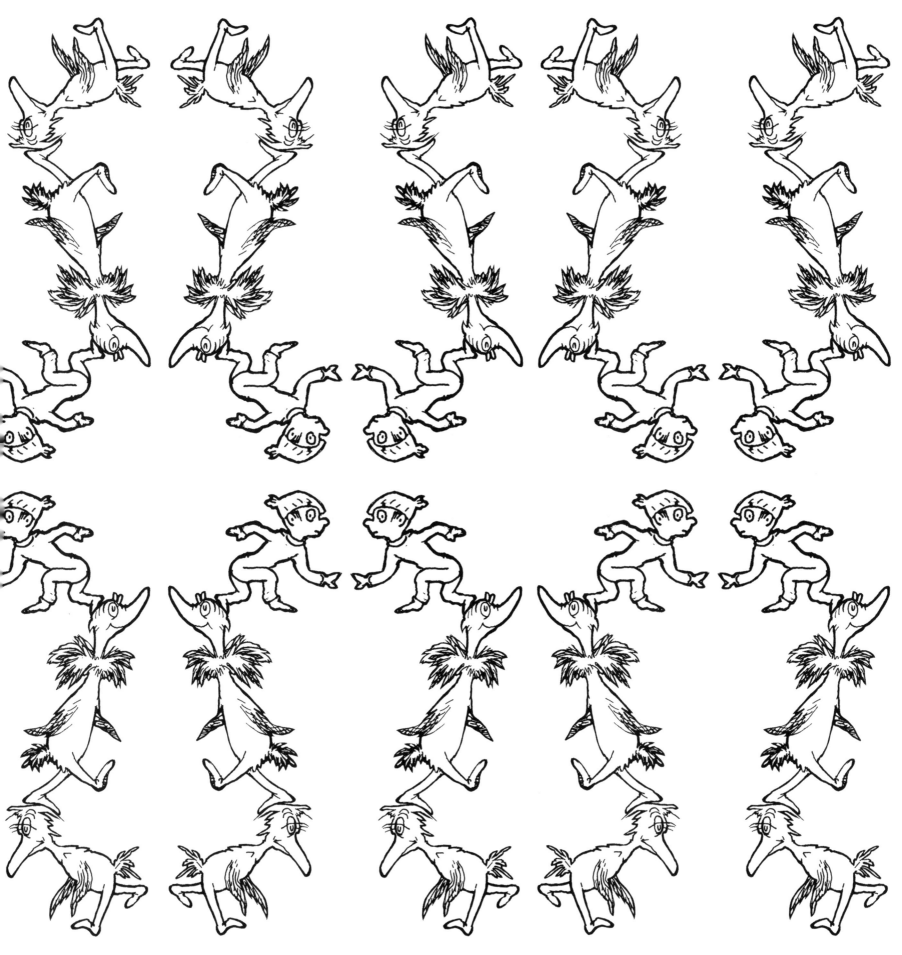

Will you succeed?

YES! You will, indeed!

(98 and 3/4 percent guaranteed.)

KID, YOU'LL MOVE MOUNTAINS!